L
AND T

Sarah Harrison
Illustrated by Kate Aldous

Hutchinson
London Melbourne Auckland Johannesburg

Just outside the village of Lark Rise, where Laura lived with her parents and her brother Edmund, stood the Big House. This was where the Squire lived, with his old mother and his wife and children. The Squire owned most of the farms around the village, and the people who lived in Lark Rise called him "our Squire" – but none of them really knew him.

"What do you think our Squire is having for his dinner?" Laura's mother would ask sometimes, as they all sat down to eat. It was a kind of game and

Laura's father, like as not, would reply rather grumpily: "Too much for his own good I shouldn't wonder."

But Laura and Edmund would suggest all kinds of things that the Squire might be eating, such as fruit cake, and joints of beef, and chocolate (which Laura had only tasted once in her life but which she had thought delicious), and wished him well of it, too.

The only time the children saw the Squire close to, was when he came once a year to play at the school concert. He was a huge, whiskery man with a bellowing laugh, and two boisterous dogs. At the concert he would play the banjo and sing, very loudly and not always in tune, though of course everyone applauded politely.

Edmund had a friend called Joe Garvey who had been caught by the Squire snaring rabbits in his woods.

Edmund made a good thing of the story. "Joe says," he would say, making it up himself, "that the Squire's face turned black, and he roared like a lion, with his eyes bulging out of his head...!"

One day Enid Sowerby had to go to the Big House to be interviewed for the job of kitchen maid. Enid was the older sister of Ella May, Laura's best friend, so they went along to keep her company. Of course Edmund wanted to go too.

"No," said Laura's mother. "You'd just be under foot."

"PLEEESE!" said Edmund.

"Oh very well," said their mother, and fetched Edmund's jacket.

Ella May was standing by her front door waiting, with Enid. Enid was twelve. Today she looked tidy and miserable, in a too-big good coat, black stockings, and a hat like a pie.

"Hallo, Laura!" said Ella May. And then: "What's he here for?"

"He's coming with us," said Laura. "Mother said he could."

"Hm!" snorted Ella May.

"Oh come *on*," called Enid plaintively.

It was nice to begin with, setting out in the early morning, but because of Enid going for the job, and wearing new stockings and her good coat, they had to walk to the Big House the long way round, by the road. It started to rain. By the time they were in sight of the tall gates they were soaked through, and their spirits were thoroughly dampened.

They trailed up the drive between

stern, dark trees. In front of them the big front door glared through the rain. Laura began to wish she hadn't come. Even Ella May seemed a lot less sure of herself than usual and Edmund had gone completely silent.

It was Enid who said: "Come on, all of you. We've got to go round the back."

The long windows of the house seemed to watch them as they trudged round, with Enid leading the way, Laura and Ella May in the middle, and Edmund trailing miserably along at the back, with his shoulders hunched.

When they got to the back door, there was a long black bell-pull, and a door-knocker in the shape of a snarling lion.

Enid looked from one to the other, the rain dripping from her hat.

"Well?" said Ella May. "Which do we do?"

"I'm thinking about it," snapped Enid.

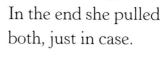 In the end she pulled both, just in case.

There was a long silence. The rain continued to pour down, hissing on their heads and shoulders, and splashing from the guttering over the door. Just when they'd decided no-one was coming and they could all go home, there were brisk footsteps inside the house, and the door opened. A pink-faced young woman in a neat, dark dress looked out at them.

"Yes, what is it?" she asked. She sounded busy.

"I'm Enid Sowerby, come about the job," said Enid in a rush. "And this is my sister, and these are my friends."

The young woman gave a sigh, and pursed her lips, but she opened the door wider and said: "Come in then, before you drown."

The three children followed her along a stone-flagged passage, leaving large wet footprints on the floor. Laura stared about her. She had never been in such an enormous house. The ceiling was so high and far away that she half expected to see clouds floating beneath it.

Through one door she saw a room lined with shelves which seemed to go on for ever, all laden with jars and crocks and tins and boxes of food, more than she'd ever seen all together in one place.

"Here we are. Take off those wet coats now. Sit down," ordered the young woman, who seemed kind in spite of her curt manner.

They had arrived in an enormous kitchen. High above them, hams in nets, and strings of onions, and bunches of dried herbs, hung like roosting bats. It was warm, and there was a delicious smell coming from a large pot which steamed gently on the black iron range.

"Would you like something to eat?" enquired the young woman.

They all nodded hard, struck dumb by their surroundings. Only Enid managed a faint "yes ma'am".

The young woman bustled about. As she did so, she asked Enid some questions about her age, and whether she could sew, and if she minded getting up early. To all of these, Enid answered "yes ma'am" or "no ma'am" according to what was expected of her.

The food arrived on the table. The children's jaws dropped. It was a feast!

There was a big cup of steaming vegetable soup for

each of them, with whole potatoes and
carrots bobbing about in it; and a whole
loaf of bread, with butter; and a big blue
and white dish with the largest joint of
cold roast beef they'd seen in their lives.
The young woman carved slices from the
joint while they sipped their soup and
watched, their eyes like saucers and their
noses damp with the steam from the soup.

After first and second helpings the three girls said no to any more, out of politeness, but Edmund was determined to eat himself to a standstill.

"Yes please!" he said, when another slice of beef was waved over his plate, and proceeded to munch his way through thirds while Enid, Ella May and Laura looked on, envious but disapproving.

"Well Enid," said the young woman briskly. "Tell your mother I'd like you to start here helping Cook on Monday next."

"Yes ma'am," replied Enid, who had more or less forgotten about the job in all the excitement of the cold beef.

"Would anyone like some fruit cake?" asked their hostess.

"Yes please," said Edmund.

It was just as Edmund had finished munching the fruit cake, and was licking his fingers to pick up the last of the currants and crumbs, that a door slammed shut upstairs. There were heavy footsteps and the clattering of dogs' paws overhead.

"Whoops, it's the Squire!" said the young woman. For the first time she seemed a little worried. "I must get busy!"

She began whisking the plates and dishes off the table. "Come along," she said to the children. "Coats on!"

A loud voice called: "What's going on in my kitchen?" The footsteps were coming down the stairs now. Laura could scarcely do her buttons up for terror.

"And who's been eating my luncheon?" boomed the voice. But the children didn't stop to answer. They were down the passage and out of the door, and down the drive as if Old Nick were after them, till they were safely back outside the gates.

Edmund was the first to recover.

"Did you ever see so much food?" he gasped.

The three girls glared at him. And he turned rather red and muttered, "Well, did you?" before running off ahead of them, up the road in the direction of Lark Rise.

After this experience Laura vowed never again to go near the Big House. The Squire was not to be trifled with. She didn't envy Enid one little bit going there to work, even though Enid said on one of her days off that she never saw the Squire anyway.

But some weeks later, Laura went for a walk near the Squire's wood. She

wanted to pick some hips and haws for
Miss Holmes at school. She went along
the side of the ploughed field at the edge
of the wood where the best bushes were.
It had been a stormy night, and the
ground was covered with broken
branches, and twigs which had been torn
off by the wind.

Suddenly, as she rounded a corner, Laura came upon a whole tree, a giant elm, lying on its side across the plough. She stared at it. It was rather sad to see such a splendid tree lying broken on the ground.

"A pitiful sight, isn't it?" asked a voice from nowhere.

Laura almost jumped out of her skin. She had thought she was alone. But now, from behind the mass of branches, appeared a tall figure. It was the Squire!

"Yes sir. It is," whispered Laura hoarsely.

The Squire patted the tree trunk almost as if it were a dog.

"I can never get used to seeing a tree felled," he said, gazing down at it. He sounded really unhappy, and to her astonishment Laura could see tears shining in his eyes.

"But – it will make lots of good firewood," she said encouragingly.

The Squire looked up at her, blinking. Laura smiled, though her heart was pounding. Had she been too forward?

But after a moment, the Squire smiled too, and nodded.

"Of course, my dear, you're absolutely right." He gave the tree trunk a final pat, as if saying good-bye. "And another one will grow in its place."

And with that he lifted his hat to
Laura, and strode off, with his two
brown and white spaniels jumping round
his legs.

Watching him go, Laura found that her heart had stopped pounding. And from then on, no matter what stories she heard about the Squire, nor how terrible his singing was, she was never frightened of him again. "After all," she'd say, "our Squire's only human."